John Carter and the Giant of Mars

Edgar Rice Burroughs

ISBN-13: 978-1475044041

ISBN-10: 1475044046

Table of Contents

Chapter One: Abduction

The moons of Mars looked down upon a giant Martian thoat as it raced silently over the soft mossy ground. Eight powerful legs carried the creature forward in great, leaping strides.

The path of the mighty beast was guided telepathically by the two people who sat in a huge saddle that was cinched to the thoat's broad back.

It was the custom of Dejah Thoris, Princess of Helium, to ride forth weekly to inspect part of her grandfather's vast farming and industrial kingdom.

Her journey to the farm lands wound through the lonely Helium Forest where grow the huge trees that furnish much of the lumber supply to the civilized nations of Mars.

Dawn was just breaking in the eastern Martian sky, and the jungle was dark and still damp with the evening dew. The gloom of the forest made Dejah Thoris thankful for the presence of her companion, who rode in the saddle in front of her. Her hands rested on his broad, bronze shoulders, and the feel of those smooth, supple muscles gave her a little thrill of confidence. One of his hands rested on the jewel-encrusted hilt of his great long sword and he sat his saddle very straight, for he was the mightiest warrior on Mars.

John Carter turned to gaze at the lovely face of his princess.

"Frightened, Dejah Thoris?" he asked.

"Never, when I am with my chieftain," Dejah Thoris smiled.

"But what of the forest monsters, the arboks?"

"Grandfather has had them all removed. On the last trip, my guard killed the only tree reptile I've ever seen."

Suddenly Dejah Thoris gasped, clutched vainly at John Carter to regain her balance. The mighty thoat lurched heavily to the mossy ground. The riders catapulted over his head. In an instant the two had regained their feet; but the thoat lay very still.

Carter jerked his long sword from its scabbard and motioned Dejah Thoris to stay at his back.

The silence of the forest was abruptly shattered by an uncanny roar directly above them.

"An arbok!" Dejah Thoris cried.

The tree reptile launched itself straight for the hated man-things. Carter lifted his sword and swung quickly to one side, drawing the monster's attention away from Dejah Thoris, who crouched behind the fallen thoat.

The earthman's first thrust sliced harmlessly through the beast's outer skin. A huge claw knocked him off balance, and he found himself lying on the ground with the great fangs at his throat.

"Dejah Thoris, get the atom gun from the thoat's back," Carter called hoarsely to the girl. There was no answer.

Calling upon every ounce of his great strength, Carter drove his sword into the arbok's neck. The creature shuddered. A stream of blood gushed from the wound. The man wriggled from under the dead body and sprang to his feet.

"Dejah Thoris! Dejah Thoris!"

Wildly Carter searched the ground and trees surrounding the dead thoat and arbok. There was no sign of Dejah Thoris. She had utterly vanished.

A shaft of light from the rising sun filtering through the foliage glistened on an object at the earthman's feet. Carter picked up a large shell, a shell recently ejected from a silent atom gun.

Springing to the dead thoat, he examined the saddle trappings. The atom gun that he had told Dejah Thoris to fire was still in its leather boot!

The earthman stooped beside the dead thoat's head. There was a tiny, bloody hole through its skull. That shot and the charging arbok had been part of a well-conceived plan to abduct Dejah Thoris, and kill him!

But Dejah Thoris--how had she disappeared so quickly, so completely?

Grimly, Carter set off at a run back to the forest toward Helium.

Noon found the earthman in a private audience chamber of Tardos Mors, Jeddak of Helium, grandfather of Dejah Thoris.

The old jeddak was worried. He thrust a rough piece of parchment into John Carter's hand. Crude, bold letters were inscribed upon the parchment; and as Carter scanned the note his eyes burned with anger. It read:

"I, Pew Mogel, the most powerful ruler on Mars, have decided to take over the iron works of Helium. The iron will furnish me with all the ships I need to protect Helium and the other cities of Barsoom from invasion. If you have not evacuated all your workers from the iron mines and factories in three days, then I will start sending you the fingers of the Royal Princess of Helium. Hurry, because I may decide to send her tongue, which wags too much of John Carter. Remember, obey Pew Mogel, for he is all-powerful."

Tardos Mors dug his nails into the palms of his hands. "Who is the upstart who calls himself the most powerful ruler of Mars?"

Carter looked thoughtfully at the note.

"He must have spies here," he said. "Pew Mogel knew that I was to leave this morning with Dejah Thoris on a tour of inspection."

"A spy it must have been," Tardos Mors groaned. "I found this note pinned to the curtains in my private audience-chamber. But what can we do? Dejah Thoris is the only thing in life that I have left to love--" His voice broke.

"All Helium loves her, Tardos Mors, and we will all die before we return to you empty-handed."

Carter strode to the visiscreen and pushed a button. "Summon Kantos Kan and Tars Tarkas." He spoke quickly to an orderly. "Have them come here at once."

Soon after, the huge, green warrior and the lean, red man were in the audience-chamber.

"It is fortunate, John Carter, that I am here in Helium on my weekly visit from the plains." Tars Tarkas, the green thark, gripped his massive sword with his powerful four hands. His great, giant body loomed majestically above the others in the room.

Kantos Kan laid his hand on John Carter's shoulder. "I was on my way to the palace when I received your summons. Already, word of our princess' abduction has spread over Helium. I came immediately," said the noble fellow, "to offer you my sword and my heart."

"I have never heard of this Pew Mogel," said Tars Tarkas. "Is he a green man?"

Tardos Mors grunted, "He's probably some petty outlaw or criminal who has an overbloated ego."

Carter raised his eyes from the ransom note.

"No, Tardos Mors, I think he is more formidable than you imagine. He is clever, also. There must have been an airship, with a silent motor, at hand to carry Dejah Thoris away so quickly--or perhaps some great bird!

Only a very powerful man who is prepared to back up his threats would kidnap the Princess of Helium and even hope to take over the great iron works.

"He probably has great resources at his command. It is doubtful, however, if he has any intention of returning the princess or he would have included more details in his ransom note."

Suddenly the earthman's keen eyes narrowed. A shadow had moved in the adjoining room.

With a powerful leap, Carter reached the arched doorway. A furtive figure melted away into the semi-gloom of the passageway, with Carter close behind.

Seeing escape impossible, the stranger halted, sank to one knee and leveled a ray-gun at the approaching figure of the earthman. Carter saw his finger whiten as he squeezed the trigger.

"Carter!" Kantos Kan shouted, "throw yourself to the floor."

With the speed of light, Carter dropped prone. A long blade whizzed over his head and buried itself to the hilt in the heart of the stranger.

"One of Pew Mogel's spies," John Carter muttered as he rose to his feet.

"Thank you, Kantos Kan."

Kantos Kan searched the body but found no clue to the man's identity. Back in the audience-chamber, the men set to work with fierce resolve. They were bending over a huge map of Barsoom when Carter spoke.

"Cities for miles around Helium are now all friendly. They would have warned us of this Pew Mogel if they had known of him. He has probably taken over one of the deserted cities in the dead sea bottom east or west of Helium. It means thousands of miles to search; but we will go over each mile."

Carter seated himself at a table and explained his plan. "Tars Tarkas, go east and contact the chiefs of all your tribes. I'll cover the west with air scouts, Kantos Kan will stay in Helium as contact man. Be ready night and day with the entire Helium air force. Whoever discovers Dejah Thoris first will notify Kantos Kan of his position. Naturally, we can only communicate to each other through Kantos Kan."

"The wave length will be constant and secret, 2000 kilocycles." Tardos Mors turned to the earthman.

"Every resource in my kingdom is at your command, John Carter."

"We leave at once, your majesty; and if Dejah Thoris is alive on Barsoom, we shall find her," replied John Carter.

Chapter Two: The Search

Within three hours, John Carter was standing on the roof of the Royal Airdrome giving last-minute instructions to a fleet of twenty-four fast, one-man scouts.

"Cover all the territory in your district thoroughly. If you discover anything, don't attempt to handle it by yourself. Notify Kantos Kan immediately." Carter surveyed the grim faces before him and knew that they would obey him.

"Let's go." Carter jerked a thumb over his shoulder to the ships.

The men scattered and soon their planes were speeding away from Helium.

Carter stayed on the roof long enough to check with Kantos Kan. He adjusted the earphones around his head and then signalled on 2000 kilocycles. The dots and dashes of Kantos Kan's reply began coming in immediately.

"Your signal comes in perfectly. Tars Tarkas is just leaving the city.

The air fleet is mobilizing. The entire air force will stand by to come to your aid. Kantos Kan signing off."

Night found Carter cruising about five hundred miles from Helium. He was very tired. The search of several ruined cities and canals had been fruitless. The buzzing of the microset aroused him again.

"Kantos Kan reporting. Tars Tarkas has organized a complete ground search east to south; other air scouts west to south report nothing. Will acquaint you with any news that might come in. Awaiting orders. Will stand by. Signing off."

"No orders. No news. Carter signing off."

Wearily he let the ship drift. No need to look further until the moons came up. The earthman fell into a fitful sleep.

It was midnight when the speaker sounded, jerking Carter to wakefulness. Kantos Kan was signalling again, excitedly.

"Tars Tarkas has found Dejah Thoris. She is held in a deserted city on the banks of the dead sea at Korvas." Kantos Kan gave the exact latitude and longitude of the spot.

"Further instructions from Tars Tarkas request the greatest secrecy in your movements. He will be at the main bridge leading into the city. Kantos Kan signing, off. Come in, John Carter."

John Carter signed off with Kantos Kan, urging him to stand by constantly to be ready with the Helium Air Fleet. Now he set his gyro-compass, a device that would automatically steer him to his destination.

Several hours later, the earthman flew over a low range of hills and saw below him an ancient city on the banks of the Dead Sea. He circled his plane and dropped to the bridge where he had been instructed to meet Tars Tarkas. Long, black shadows filled a dry gully below him.

Carter climbed out of his plane, keeping to the shadows, and made his way to the towering ruins of the city. It was so quiet that a lonely bat swooping from a tower sounded like a falling airship.

Where was Tars Tarkas? The green man should have appeared at the bridge.

At the entrance to the city, Carter stepped into the black shadow of a wall and waited. No sound broke the stillness of the quiet night. The city was like a tomb. Diemos and Phobos, the two fast-moving moons of Mars, whirled across the heavens.

Carter stopped breathing to listen. To his keen ears came the faint sound of steps--strange, shuffling steps dragging closer.

Something was coming along the wall. The earthman tensed, ready to spring away to his ship. Now he could hear other steps all around him. Inside the ruins something dragged against the fallen rocks.

Then a great, heavy body dropped on John Carter from the wall above. Hot, fetid breath burned his neck. Huge, shaggy arms smothered him in their fierce embrace.

The thing hurled him to the rough cobblestones. Huge hands clutched at his throat. Carter turned his head and saw above him the face of a great, white ape.

Three of the creature's fellows were circling around Carter, striving to tie his feet with a piece of rope while the other choked him into insensibility with his four mighty hands.

Carter wriggled his feet under the belly of the ape with whom he was grappling. One mighty heave sent the creature into the air to fall, groaning and helpless, to the ground.

Like a cornered banth (the huge, eight-legged lion of Mars. Ed.), Carter was on his feet, crouched against the wall, awaiting the attacking trio, with drawn sword.

They were mighty beasts, fully eight feet tall with long, white hair covering their great bodies. Each was equipped with four muscular arms that ended in tremendous hands armed with sharp, hooked claws. They were baring their fangs and growling viciously as they came toward the earthman.

Carter crouched low; and as the beasts sprang in, his earthly muscles sent him leaping high into the air over their heads. The earthman's heavy blade, backed by all the power of his muscles, smacked down upon one ape's head, splitting the skull wide open.

Carter hit the ground and, turning, was ready when the two apes remaining flew at him again. There was a hideous, hair-raising shriek as this time the earthman's sword sank deep into a savage heart.

As the monster sprawled to the ground, the earthman jerked free his sword.

Now the other beast turned and slunk away in fright, his eyes gleaming at Carter in the darkness as it fled down a long corridor in the adjacent building. The earthman could have sworn that he heard his own name coming from the ape's throat and mingling with its sullen growl as it fled away.

The earthman had just seized his sword when he felt a rush of air above his head. There was a blur of motion as something came down toward him.

Now he felt himself clutched about the waist; then he was jerked fifty feet into the air. Struggling for breath, Carter clutched at the thing encircling his body. It was as horny as the skin of an arbok. It had hairs as large as tree roots bristling from the horny scales. It was a giant hand!

Chapter Three: Joog - The Giant

John Carter found himself looking into a monstrous face. From top of shaggy head to bottom of its hairy chin, the head measured fully fifteen feet.

A new monstrosity had come to life on Mars. Judging by the adjacent buildings, the creature must have been a hundred and thirty feet tall!

The giant raised Carter high over his head and shook him; then he threw back his face. Hideous, hollow laughter rumbled out of his pendulous lips revealing teeth like small mountain crags.

He was dressed in an ill-fitting, baggy tunic that came down in loose folds over his hips but which allowed his arms and legs to be free.

With his other hand he beat his mighty chest.

"I, Joog. I, Joog," he kept repeating as he continued to laugh and shake his helpless victim. "I can kill! I can kill!" Joog, the giant, commenced to walk. Carefully he stepped along the barren streets, sometimes going around a building that was too high to step over. Finally he stopped before a partially ruined palace. The ravages of time had only dimmed its beauty. Huge masses of moss and vines trailed through the masonry, hiding the shattered battlements. With a sudden thrust, Joog, the giant, shoved John Carter through a high window in the palace tower.

When Carter felt the giant's hold releasing upon him he relaxed completely. He hit the stone floor in a long roll, protecting his head with his arms. As he lay in the deep darkness of the place where he had fallen, the earthman listened while he regained his breath.

No sound came to his ears for some time; then he began to hear the heavy breathing of Joog outside his window. Once more Carter's earthly muscles, reacting to the lesser gravity of Mars, sent him leaping twenty feet to the sill of the narrow window. Here he clung and looked once again into the hairy, hideous face of the giant.

"I, Joog. I, Joog," he mumbled. "I can kill! I can kill!" The giant's breath swept over Carter like a blast from a sulphur furnace. There would be no escape from that window!

Once more he dropped down into his cell. This time he commenced a slow circuit of the room, groping his way along the polished ersite slabs that formed the wall. The cobblestone floor was thick with debris. Once, Carter heard the sinister hiss of a Martian spider as he brushed its web.

How long he groped his way around the walls, there was no way of knowing. It seemed hours. Then, suddenly, the deathly silence was shattered by a woman's scream coming from somewhere in the building.

John Carter could feel his skin grew cold. Could that have been the voice of Dejah Thoris?

Once again John Carter leaped toward the faint light that marked the window ledge. Cautiously, he looked down. Joog lay on his back on the flagstones below, breathing as though he were asleep, his great chest rising five feet with every breath. Quietly he started to edge his way along a ledge that ran from the window and disappeared into the shadow of an adjoining tower. If he could make that shadow without awakening Joog!

He had almost gained his objective when Joog growled hoarsely.

He had opened one great eye. Now he reached up and, grabbing Carter by the leg, hurled him into the tower window again.

Wearily, the earthman crawled to the wall of his dark cell and there slumped down against it. That scream haunted his memory. He was tormented by the thought that Dejah Thoris might be in danger.

And where was Tars Tarkas? Pew Mogel must have captured him, too. Carter suddenly sprang to his feet.

One of the ersite slabs at his back had moved! He waited. Nothing came out. Cautiously, he approached the rock and shoved it with his foot. The slab moved slightly inward. Now Carter shoved the stone with all his tremendous strength. Inch by inch he moved it until finally there was room for him to squeeze his body through.

He was still in utter darkness, but his gripping fingers revealed to him that he was in a corridor between two walls. Perhaps this was the way out of his prison!

Carefully he shoved the stone back into position, leaving no trace of his disappearance from the room. The corridor in which he found himself was so low that he was forced to crawl on hands and knees. The low corridor had the stench of age, as if it had been unused for a long time.

Gradually the tunnel sloped more and more downward. Many little side-passages branched off from the main tunnel. There was no light, no noise. Only a faint, pungent odor beginning to fill the air.

Now it was growing lighter. The earthman realized that he must be in the subterranean caverns of the palace. The dim light was caused by the phosphorescent radium glow that is used on all Mars for radiation.

The source of this faint light the earthman suddenly discovered. It was shining through a cleft in the wall ahead. Pushing aside another loose stone, John Carter crawled forth into a chamber. He drew in his breath sharply.

Facing him was a warrior with drawn sword, the point of which was almost touching the breast of the earthman! John Carter leaped back with the speed of lightning, whipped out his own sword and struck at the other's weapon.

The arm of the red man fell from his body to the floor where it dissolved into dust. The ancient sword clattered on the cobblestones.

Carter could see now that the warrior had been leaning against the wall, balanced there precariously for ages, his sword arm extending in front of him just as it had stiffened long ago in death. The loss of the arm overbalanced the torso which toppled to the floor and there dissolved into a heap of ash-like dust!

In an adjoining chamber there were a score of women, beautiful girls, chained together by collars of gold around their necks. They sat at a table where they had been eating, and the food was still before them. They had been the prisoners, the slaves of the rulers of the long-dead city. The dry, motionless air combined with some gaseous secretion from the walls and dungeons had preserved their beauty through the ages.

The earthman had traversed some little distance down a musty corridor when he became aware of something scraping behind him. Whirling into a side corridor he looked back. Gleaming eyes were coming toward him. They followed him as he backed into the tunnel.

Now again came the scraping, repeated this time farther ahead in the tunnel. Other eyes shone ahead of him.

John Carter ran forward, his sword-point extended. The eyes ahead retreated, but those in back of him started to close.

It was very dark now, but far ahead the earthman could see a faint gleam of light filtering into the tunnel.

He ran toward the light. Fighting the things where he could see them would be a lot easier than stumbling around in a dark corridor.

Carter entered the room and in the dim light came face to face with the creature whose eyes he had seen ahead of him in the tunnel It was a species of the huge three-legged Martian rat!

Its yellow fangs were bared hideously in a vicious snarl, as it backed slowly away from Carter to the far end of the small room.

Now behind him came the other rat, and together the two beasts started to close in upon the earthman.

Carter smiled grimly as he gripped his sword. "I am the proverbial cornered rat now," he muttered as he swung his blade at the nearest creature.

It ducked the blow and scurried toward him.

But the earthman's sword was ready. The charging rat lunged full upon the waiting sword-point.

The momentum of the beast carried Carter back five feet; but he still retained a hold on his sword, the point of which had plunged through the animal's single shoulder and pierced its wild heart.

When Carter had jerked free his sword and turned to meet his other antagonist an exclamation of dismay escaped his lips. The room was half filled with rats!

The creatures had entered through another opening and had formed a circle around him, waiting to attack.

For half an hour, Carter battled furiously for his life in the lonely dungeon beneath the palace in the ancient city of Korvas.

The carcasses of the dead rats were piled high around him, but still they came and eventually they overpowered him by their very numbers.

John Carter went down by a terrific blow to his head from a snake-like tail.

He was half stunned, but he still clung tenaciously to his sword as he felt himself seized by the arms and dragged away into the darkness of an adjoining tunnel.

Chapter Four: The City of Rats

John Carter recovered fully when he was dragged through a pool of muddy water. He heard the rats greedily drinking, saw their green eyes gleaming in the darkness. The smell of freshly dug earth reached his nostrils and he realized that he was in a burrow far under the subterranean vaults of the palace.

Several rats on either side of him had hold of his arms by their forepaws as they dragged him along. It was very uncomfortable, and he wondered how much longer the journey would last.

Nor had he long to wait. The strange company finally came out into a huge underground cavern. Light from the outside filtered down through various openings in the ceiling above, its rays reflecting on thousands of gleaming stalactites of red sandstone. Massive stalagmites, huge sedimentary formations of grotesque shape, rose up from the floor of the cavern.

Among these formations on the floor were numerous dome-shaped mud huts.

As Carter was dragged by, he stared at a hut that several rats were constructing. The framework was composed of white sticks of various shapes plastered with mud from an underground stream bed. The white sticks were very irregular in length and size. One of the rats stopped work to gnaw at a stick. It looked like a bone.

As he was dragged closer, he saw that the stick was a human thigh bone!

The mud huts were studded with bones and skulls, upon some of which were still dangling hideously the vestiges of hair and skin. Carter noticed that the tops of all the skulls had been removed, neatly sliced off.

The earthman was dragged to a clearing in the center of the cavern. Here, upon a mound of skulls, sat a rat half again as large as the others.

The baleful, pink eyes of the creature glared at Carter as he was dragged up on top of the mound.

The beasts released their hold upon the earthman and descended to the bottom of the mound, leaving Carter alone with the large rat.

The long whiskers of the monster were constantly twitching as the thing sniffed at the man. It had lost one ear in some battle long ago and the other was bright with scar-tissue.

Its little pink eyes surveyed Carter for a long time while it fondly caressed its long, hairless tail with its one claw-like paw. This, evidently, was the King of the Rats.

"Lord of the Underworld," Carter thought, trying to hold his breath. The stench in the cavern was overwhelming.

Without taking his eyes from Carter's, the rat reached down and picked up a skull beside him and put it in front of Carter. This he repeated, picking up a skull from the other side and placing it beside the first. By repeating this, he eventually formed a little ring of topless heads in front of the earth-man.

Now, very judiciously, he climbed inside the circle of skulls and picking one of them up tossed it to Carter. The earthman caught it and tossed it back at the king.

This seemed to annoy his royal highness. He made no effort to catch the skull and it flew past him and went bouncing down the mound.

Instead, the king leaped up and down inside the little circle of skulls, at the same time emitting angry squeals. This was all very puzzling to the earthman. As he stood there, he became aware of two circles of rats forming at the base of the mound, each circle consisting of about a thousand animals. They began a weird dance, moving around the raised dais of bones counter-clockwise. The tail of each rat was gripped in the mouth of the following beast, thus forming a continuous chain.

There was no doubt that the earthman was in the center of a weird ritual. While he was ignorant of the exact nature of the ceremony, he had little doubt as to its final outcome. The countless barren skulls, the yellowed ones that filled the cavern were mute, horrible evidence of his final fate.

Where did the rats get all the bodies from which the skulls were obtained and why were the tops of those skulls missing? The City of Korvas, as every Martian schoolboy knew, had been deserted for a thousand years; yet many of the skulls and bones were recently picked clean of their flesh. Carter had seen no evidence in the city of any life other than the great white apes and the mysterious giant, and the rats themselves. However, there had been the woman's scream that he had heard earlier. This thought accentuated his ever-present anxiety over Dejah Thoris's safety and whereabouts.

This delay was tormenting. As the circles of rats closed in about him, the earthman's eyes eagerly searched for some avenue of escape.

The rats circled slowly, watching their king, who rose to his hind legs stamping his feet, thumping his tail. The mound of skulls echoed hollowly.

Faster danced the king and faster moved the circles of rats drawing ever closer to the mound.

The closer rats shot hungry glances at the earthman. Carter smiled grimly and gripped his sword more tightly. Strange that they should let him retain it.

More than one of the beasts would die before he was overcome, and the king would be the first to go. There was no doubt that he was to be sacrificed to furnish a gastronomic orgy.

Suddenly the king stopped his wild gyrations directly in front of Carter. The dancers halted instantly, watching, waiting.

A strange, growling squeal started deep in the king's throat and grew in volume to an ear-piercing shriek. The King of Rats stepped over the ring of skulls and advanced slowly toward Carter.

Once again the earthman glanced about seeking some means of escape from the mound. This time he looked up. The ceiling was at least fifty feet away. No native-born Martian would ever consider escaping in that direction.

But John Carter had been born on the planet Earth, and he had brought with him to Mars all the strength and agility of a trained athlete.

It was upon this, combined with the lesser gravity of Mars, that the earthman made his quick plan for the next moment. Tensely he waited for his opportunity. The ceremony was nearly concluded. The king was baring his fangs not a foot from Carter's neck.

The earthman's hand tightened on his sword-hilt; then the blade streaked from its scabbard. There was a blur of motion and a sickening smack. The king's head flew into the air and then rolled away, bouncing down the mound.

The other beasts beneath were stunned into silence, but only momentarily. Now, squealing wildly, they swarmed up the mount intent on tearing the earthman to pieces.

John Carter crouched and with a mighty leap his earthly muscles sent him shooting fifty feet up into the air.

Desperately he clutched and held to a hanging stalactite. Soon he was swinging on the hanging moss to the vast upper reaches of the cavern.

Once he looked down to see the rats milling and squealing in confusion beneath. One other fact he noted, also. Apparently there was only one means of entrance or exit into the dungeon that formed the rats' underground city, the same tunnel through which he had first been dragged.

Now, however, the earthman was intent upon finding some means of exit in the ceiling above.

At last he found a narrow opening; and plunging through a heavy curtain of moss Carter swung into a cave. There were several tunnels branching off into the darkness, most of them thickly hung with the sticky webs of the great Martian spider. They were evidently parts of a vast underground network of tunnels that had been fashioned long ages ago by the ancients who once inhabited Korvas.

Carter was ready with his blade for any encounter with man or beast that might come his way; and so he started off up the largest tunnel.

The perpetually burning radium light that had been set in the wall when the tunnel was constructed furnished sufficient illumination for the earthman to see his way quite clearly.

Carter halted before a massive door set into the end of a tunnel. It was inscribed with hieroglyphics unfamiliar to the earthman. The subdued drone of what sounded like many motors seemed to come from somewhere beyond the door.

He pushed open the unbarred door and halted just beyond, staring unbelievingly at the tremendous laboratory in which he found himself.

Great motors pumped oxygen through low pipes into rows of glass cages that lined the walls and filled the antiseptically white chamber from end to end. In the center of the laboratory were several operating tables with large searchlights focused down upon them from above.

But the contents of the glass cages immediately absorbed the earthman's attention.

Each cage contained a giant white ape, standing upright inside, apparently lifeless.

The top of each hairy head was swathed in bandages. If these beasts were dead, why then the oxygen tubes running to their cages?

Carter moved across the room to examine the cases at closer range. Halfway to the farther wall he came upon a low, glassed dome that covered a huge pit set in the floor.

He gasped. The pit was filled with dead bodies, red warriors with the tops of their heads neatly sliced off!

Chapter Five: Chamber of Horrors

Far below, in the pit, John Carter could see forms moving in and about the bodies of the dead red men.

They were rats; and as he watched the earthman could see them dragging bodies off into adjoining tunnels. These tunnels probably entered the main one which ran into the rats' underground city.

So this was where the beasts got the skulls and bones with which they constructed their odorous, underground dwellings!

Carter's eyes scanned the laboratory. He noted the operating tables, the encased instruments above, the anesthetics. Everything pointed to some grisly experiment, conducted by some insane scientist.

Within a glass case were many books. One ponderous volume was inscribed in gold letters: PEW MOGEL, HIS LIFE AND WONDERFUL WORKS.

The earthman frowned. What was the explanation? Why this well-equipped laboratory buried in an ancient lost city, a city apparently deserted except for apes, rats, and a giant man?

Why the cases about the wall containing the mute, motionless bodies of apes with bandaged heads? And the red men in the pit--why were their skulls cut in half, their brains removed?

From whence came the giant, the monstrous creature whose likeness had existed only in the Barsoomian folklore?

One of the books in a case before Carter bore the name "Pew Mogel." What connection had Pew Mogel with all this and who was the man?

But more important, where was Dejah Thoris, the Princess of Helium?

John Carter reached for Pew Mogel's book. Suddenly the room fell silent. The generators that had been humming out their power, stopped.

"Touch not that book, John Carter," came the words echoing through the laboratory.

Carter's hand dropped to his sword. There was a moment's pause; then the hidden voice continued.

"Give yourself up, John Carter, or your princess dies." The words were apparently coming from a concealed loudspeaker somewhere in the room.

"Through the door to your right, earthman, the door to your right."

Carter immediately sensed a trap. He crossed to the door. Warily, he pushed it open with his foot.

Upon a gorgeous throne at the far end of a huge dome-shaped chamber sat a hideous, misshapen man. A tiny, bullet head squatted upon massive shoulders.

Everything about the creature seemed distorted. His torso was crooked, his arms were not equal in length; one foot was larger than the other.

The face in the diminutive head leered at John Carter. A thick tongue hung partly out over yellowed teeth.

The hulking body was encased in gorgeous trappings of platinum and diamonds. One claw-like hand stroked the bare head.

From head to foot there was apparently not a hair on his body.

At the man's feet crouched a great, four-armed shaggy brute--another white ape. Its little red eyes were fixed steadily upon the earthman as he stood at the far end of the chamber. The man on the throne idly fingered the microphone with which he had summoned Carter to the room.

"I have trapped you at last, John Carter!" Beady, cocked eyes glared with hatred. "You cannot cope with the great brain of Pew Mogel!"

Pew Mogel turned to a television screen studded with dials and lights of various colors.

His face twisted into a smile. "You honor my humble city, John Carter. It is with the greatest interest I have watched your progress through the many chambers of the palace with my television machine." Pew Mogel patted the machine.

"This little invention of my good teacher, Ras Thavas," continued Pew Mogel, "which I acquired from him, has been an invaluable aid to me in learning of your intended search for my unworthy person. It was unfortunate that you should suspect the honorable intentions of my agent that afternoon in the jeddak's chambers.

"Fortunately, however, he had already completed his mission; and through an extension upon this television set, concealed cleverly behind a mirror in the jeddak's private throne room, I was able to see and hear the entire proceedings."

Pew Mogel laughed vacantly, his little unblinking eyes staring steadily at Carter who remained motionless at the other end of the room.

The earthman could see nothing in the chamber that indicated a trap. The walls and floor were all of grey, polished ersite slabs. Carter stood at one end of a long aisle leading to Pew Mogel's throne.

Slowly he advanced toward Pew Mogel, his hand grasping his sword, the muscles of his arm etched bands of steel.

Halfway down the aisle, the earthman halted. "Where is Dejah Thoris?" His words cut the air.

The microcephalic head (A microcephalic head is one possessing a very small brain capacity. It is the opposite of megacephalic, which means a large brain capacity) of Pew Mogel cocked to one side. Carter waited for him to speak.

Generally microcephalia is a sign of idiocy, although in the case of Pew Mogel, the condition did not mean idiocy, but extreme craftiness, and madness, which might indicate that, since Pew Mogel was an artificial, synthetic product of Ras Thavas, one of Mars's most famous scientists, his microcephalia was either caused by a disease, or by inability of the brain to adapt itself to a foreign ill-fitting cranial cavity. Pew Mogel's head was obviously too small for his body, or for his brain. Ed.

In spite of having the features of a man, Pew Mogel did not look quite human. There was something indescribably repulsive about him, the thin lips, the hollow cheeks, the close-set eyes.

Then Carter realized that those eyes were unblinking. There were no eyelids. The man's eyes could never close. Pew Mogel spoke coldly. "I am greatly indebted to you for this visit. I was fortunate enough to be able to entertain your princess and your best friend; but I hardly dared to hope you would honor me, too."

Carter's face was expressionless. Slowly he repeated, "Where is Dejah Thoris?"

Pew Mogel leered mockingly.

The earthman advanced toward the throne. The white ape at Pew Mogel's feet growled, the hairs on its neck bristling upright as Pew Mogel flinched slightly.

Again the twisted smile passed over his face as he raised his hand toward John Carter and drawled.

"Have patience, John Carter, and I will show you your princess; but first, perhaps you will be interested in seeing the man who, last night, told you to meet him at the main bridge outside the city."

Pew Mogel's left eye suddenly popped out of its socket and dangled on his cheek. He took no notice of it, but continued to speak, glancing first at Carter and then at Tars Tarkas with the other eye.

"You have both met Joog," stated Pew Mogel. "One hundred and thirty feet tall, he is all muscle, a product of science, the result of my great brain."

Pew Mogel hooked one of his fingers over a lever projecting from the golden arm of his throne and slipped it toward himself. A pillar to the left of his throne, half set in the wall, began to revolve slowly.

A giant green man appeared, chained to the pillar. His four mighty arms were strapped securely; and for Pew Mogel's additional safety, several steel chains were wrapped around his body and cinched with massive padlocks. His neck and ankles were also secured with bands of steel, also padlocked.

"Tars Tarkas!" Carter exclaimed.

"Kaor, John Carter," there was a grim smile on Tars Tarkas's face as he replied. "I see our friend here trapped us both the same way; but it took a giant fifteen times my size to hold me while they trussed me in these chains."

"The message you sent me last night--" In a flash, Carter realized the truth. Pew Mogel had faked the messages from Kantos Kan and Tars Tarkas, trapping them both in the city the night before.

"Yes, I sent you both identical messages," said Pew Mogel, "each message apparently from the other. The proper broadcasting length I ascertained from listening to the concealed microphone I had planted in the jeddak's throne room. Clever. With my own hands I created him from living flesh, the greatest fighting monster that Barsoom has ever seen. I modeled him from the organs, tissues, and bones of ten thousand red men and white apes."

Pew Mogel, becoming aware of his left eye, quickly shoved it back into place.

Tars Tarkas laughed one of his rare laughs. "Pew Mogel," he said, "you are falling apart. As you claim to have created your giant, so you yourself have been made.

"Unless I miss my guess, John Carter," continued Tars Tarkas, "this freak before us who calls himself a king has, himself, crawled out of a tissue vat!"

Pew Mogel's pallid countenance turned even paler as he leaped to his feet. He struck Tars Tarkas a vicious blow on the face.

"Silence, green man!" he shrieked.

Tars Tarkas only smiled at this insult, ignoring the pain. John Carter's face was a frozen mask. One more blow at his defenseless friend would have sent him at Pew Mogel's throat.

Better to bide his time, he knew, until he learned where Dejah Thoris was hidden.

Pew Mogel sank back upon his throne. The white ape, who had risen, once more squatted down at his master's feet.

Presently Pew Mogel smiled again. "So sorry," he drawled, "that I lost my temper. Sometimes I forget that my present appearance reveals the nature of my origin.

"You see, soon I shall have trained one of my apes in the intricate procedure of transferring my marvelous brain into a suitable, handsome body; then no one will guess that I am not like any other normal man on Barsoom."

John Carter smiled grimly at Pew Mogel's words. "Then you are one of Ras Thavas's synthetic men?"

Chapter Six: Pew Mogel

"Yes, I am a synthetic man," answered Pew Mogel slowly. "My brain was the greatest achievement of all The Master Mind's creations.

"For years I was a devoted pupil of Ras Thavas in his laboratories at Morbus. I learned all that the Master could teach me of the secrets of creating living tissue. When I learned from him all that I thought necessary to pursue my plans, I left Morbus. With a hundred synthetic men I escaped over the Great Toonolian Marshes on the backs of malagors, the birds of transport.

"I brought with me all the intricate equipment that I could steal from his laboratories. The rest, I have fashioned here in this ancient deserted city where we finally landed."

John Carter was studying Pew Mogel intently.

"I was tired of being a slave," continued Pew Mogel. "I wanted to rule; and by Issus, I have ruled; and some day I shall rule all Barsoom!"

Pew Mogel's eyes gleamed.

"It was not long before red men gathered in our city, escaped and exiled criminals. Since their faces would only lead them to capture and execution in other civilized cities on Barsoom, I persuaded them to allow me to transfer their brains into the bodies of the stupid white apes that overran this city.

"I promised to later restore their brains into the bodies of other red men, provided they would help me in my conquests."

Carter recalled the apes with the bandaged heads in the adjoining laboratory, and the red men with their skulls sliced off in the chamber of the rats. He began to understand a little; then he remembered Joog. "But the giant?" asked John Carter. "Whence came he?"

Pew Mogel was silent for a minute; then he spoke.

"Joog I have built, piece by piece, during several years, from the bones, tissues and organs of a thousand red men and white apes who came voluntarily to me or whom I captured.

"Even his brain is the synthesis of the brains of ten thousand red men and white apes. Into Joog's veins I have pumped a serum that makes all tissues self-repairing.

"My giant is practically indestructible. No bullet or cannon-shot made can stop him!"

Pew Mogel smiled and stroked his hairless chin. "Think how powerful my ape soldiers will be," he purred, "each one armed with the great strength of an ape. With their four arms they can hold twice as many weapons as ordinary men, and inside their skulls will function the cunning brains of human beings.

"With Joog and my army of white apes, I can go forth and become master of all Barsoom." Pew Mogel paused and then added, "provided I acquire more iron for even greater weapons than I already have."

Now Pew Mogel had risen from his throne in his great excitement.

"I preferred to conquer peacefully by first acquiring the Helium iron works as payment for Dejah Thoris's safe return. But the jeddak and John Carter force me into other alternatives. However, I'll give you one more chance to settle peacefully," he said.

Pew Mogel's hand moved toward the right arm of his throne, as he pulled a duplicate lever. A beautiful woman swung into view.

It was Dejah Thoris!

At the sight of his princess chained to the other pillar before him John Carter grew very pale. He sprang forward to free her.

His earthly muscles could have easily covered the distance in one leap; but halfway there in his spring, Dejah Thoris and Tars Tarkas saw the earthman sprawl in midair as though he had struck full force against some invisible barrier. Half-stunned, he crumpled to the floor.

Dejah Thoris gave a little cry. Tars Tarkas strained at his bonds. Slowly, the earthman rose to his feet, shaking his body like some majestic animal. With his sword he reached down and felt the barrier that stood between him and the throne. Pew Mogel laughed harshly.

"You are trapped, John Carter. The invisible glass partition that you struck is another invention of the great Ras Thavas that I acquired. It is invulnerable.

"From there, you may watch the torture of your princess, unless she sees fit to sign a note to her father demanding the surrender of Helium to me."

The earthman looked at his princess not ten feet from him. Dejah Thoris held her head proudly high, which was answer enough to Pew Mogel's demands that she betray her people.

Pew Mogel saw, and angrily issued a command to the ape. The white brute rose and ambled over to Dejah Thoris. Grabbing her hair with one paw, he forced her head back until he could see her face. His hideous grinning face was not two inches from hers.

"Demand Helium's surrender," hissed Pew Mogel, "and you shall have your freedom!"

"Never!" the word shot back at him.

Pew Mogel flung another command to the ape.

The creature planted his great, pendulous lips on those of the princess. Dejah Thoris went limp in his embrace, while Tars Tarkas surged vainly at the steel chains. The girl had fainted.

The earthman again hurled himself futilely against the barrier that he could not see.

"Fool," yelled Pew Mogel, "I gave you your chance to retain your princess by turning over to me the Helium iron works; but you and the jeddak thought you could thwart me and regain Dejah Thoris without paying me the price I asked for her safe return. For that mistake, you all die."

Pew Mogel again reached over to the instrument board beside his throne. He began to turn several dials, and Carter heard a strange, droning noise that increased steadily in volume.

Suddenly the earthman turned and raced for the door through which he came.

But before he had covered fifteen feet, another barrier had closed down. Escape through the door was impossible.

There was a window over on the wall to his right. He leaped for it. He struck another glass barrier.

There was another window on the left side of the room. He had nearly reached it when he was met by another wall of invisible glass.

In a flash he became acutely conscious of his predicament. The walls were moving in upon him. He could see now that the glass barriers had moved out from cleverly concealed slits in the adjoining walls.

The two side barriers, however, were fastened to horizontal pistons in the ceiling. These pistons were moving together, bringing the glass walls toward each other, and would eventually crush the earthman between them. Upon John Carter's finger was a jeweled ring. Set in the center of the ring was a large diamond. Diamonds can cut glass!

Here was a new type of glass, but the chances were it was not as hard as the diamond on Carter's finger!

The earthman clenched his fist, pressed the diamond ring against the barrier in front of him and quickly made a large circular scratch in the glass surface.

Then he crashed his body with all his strength against the area of glass enclosed by the scratch.

The section broke out neatly at the blow, and the earthman found himself face to face with Pew Mogel.

Dejah Thoris had regained consciousness, a set, intent expression on her beautiful face. A grim smile had settled over Tars Tarkas's lips when he saw that his friend was no longer impeded by the invisible barriers.

Pew Mogel shrank back on his throne and gasped in a cracked voice.

"Seize him, Gore, seize him!" Little beads of sweat stood forth on his brow.

Gore, the white ape, released his hold on Dejah Thoris and, turning, saw the earthman advancing toward them. Gore snarled viciously, revealing jagged, mighty fangs. He crouched low, so that his four massive fists supported his weight on the floor. His little, beady, blood-shot eyes gleamed hatred, for Gore hated all men save Pew Mogel.

Chapter Seven: The Flying Terror

As Gore, the great white ape with a man's brain, crouched to meet John Carter, he was fully confident of overcoming his puny man opponent.

But to make assurance doubly sure, Gore drew the great blade at his side and rushed madly at his foe, hacking and cutting viciously.

The momentum of the brute's attack forced Carter backward a few steps as he deftly warded off the mighty blows.

But the earthman saw his chance. Quickly, surely, his blade streaked. There was a sudden twist and Gore's sword went hurtling across the room. Gore, however, reacted with lightning speed. With his four huge hands he grasped the naked steel of the earthman's sword.

Violently he jerked the blade from Carter's grasp and, raising it overhead, snapped the strong steel in two as if it had been a splinter of wood.

Now, with a low growl, Gore closed in; and Carter crouched.

Suddenly the man leaped over the ape's head; but again with uncanny speed the monster shot out a hairy hand and grasped the earthman's ankle.

Gore held John Carter in his four hands, drawing the man closer and closer to the drooling jowls and gleaming fangs.

But with a surge of his mighty muscles, the earthman jerked free his arm and sent a terrific blow crashing full into Gore's face.

The ape recoiled, dropping John Carter, and staggered back toward the huge window on the right wall by Pew Mogel's throne.

Here the beast tottered; and the earthman, seeing his chance, once again leaped into the air, but this time flew feet foremost toward the ape.

At the moment of contact with the ape's chest, Carter extended his legs violently; and so, as his feet struck Gore, this force was added to the hurtling momentum of his body.

With a bellowing cry, Gore hurtled out through the window and his screams ended only when he landed with a sickening crunch in the courtyard far below.

Dejah Thoris and Tars Tarkas, chained to the pillars, had watched the short fight, fascinated by the earthman's sure, quick actions.

But when Carter did not succumb instantly to Gore's attack, Pew Mogel had grown frightened. He began jerking dials and switches; and then spoke swiftly into the little microphone beside him.

So now, as the earthman regained his feet and advanced slowly toward Pew Mogel, he did not see the black shadow that obscured the window behind him.

Only when Dejah Thoris screamed a warning did the earthman turn. But he was too late!

A giant hand, fully three feet across, closed about his body. He was lifted from the floor and pulled out quickly through the window.

To Carter's ears came the hopeless cry of his princess mingled with the cruel, hollow laugh of Pew Mogel.

Carter did not need the added assurance of his eyes to know that he was being held in the grasp of Pew Mogel's synthetic giant. Joog's fetid breath blasting across his face was ample evidence.

Joog held Carter several feet from his face and contracted his features in the semblance of a grin, exposing his two great rows of cracked, stained teeth the size of sharp boulders. Hoarse, gurgling sounds emanated from Joog's throat as he held the earthman before his face.

"I, Joog. I, Joog," the monster finally managed. "I can kill! I can kill!"

Then he shook his victim until the man's teeth rattled. But quite suddenly the giant was quiet, listening; then Carter became aware of muffled words coming, apparently, from Joog's ear.

Then John Carter realized that the command was coming from Pew Mogel, transmitted by short wave to a receiving device attached to one of Joog's ears.

"To the arena," repeated the voice. "Fasten him over the pit!"

The pit--what new form of devilish torture was this? Carter tried vaguely to ease the awful pressure that was crushing him. But his arms were pinned to his sides by the giant's grasp. All the man could do was breathe laboriously and hope that Joog's great strides would soon bring them to his destination, whatever that might be.

The giant's tremendous pace, stepping over tall, ancient edifices or across wide, spacious plazas in single, mighty strides, soon brought them to a large, crowded amphitheatre on the outskirts of the city.

The amphitheatre apparently was fashioned from a natural crater. Row upon row of circular tiers had been carved within the inner wall of the crater, forming a series of levels upon which sat thousands of white apes.

In the center of the arena was a circular pit about fifty feet across. The pit contained what appeared to be water whose level was about fifteen feet from the top of the pit.

Three iron-barred cages hung suspended over the center of the pit by means of three heavy ropes, one attached to the top of each cage and running up through a pulley in the scaffolding built overhead and down to the edge of the pit where it was anchored. Joog climbed partly over the edge of the coliseum and deposited Carter on the brink of the pit. Five great apes held him there while another ape lowered one of the cages to ground level.

Then he reached out with a hooked pole and swung the cage over the edge. He unlocked the cage door with a large key.

The keeper for the key was a short, heavy-set ape with a bull neck and exceedingly close-set eyes.

This brute now came up to Carter and although the captive was being held by five other apes, he grabbed him cruelly by the hair and jerked Carter into the cage, at the same time kicking him viciously.

The cage door was slammed immediately, it's padlock bolted closed. Now Carter's cage was pulled up over the pit and the rope anchored to a davit at the edge.

It was not long before Joog returned with Dejah Thoris and Tars Tarkas. Their chains had been removed.

They were placed in the other two cages that hung over the pit next to John Carter.

"Oh, John Carter, my chieftain!" cried Dejah Thoris, when she saw him in the cage next to hers. "Thank Issus you are still alive!" The little princess was crying softly.

John Carter reached through the bars and took her hand in his. He tried to speak reassuring words to her but he knew, as did Tars Tarkas, who sat grim faced in the other cage beside his, that Pew Mogel had ordained their deaths--but in what manner they would die, Carter, as yet, was uncertain.

"John Carter," spoke Tars Tarkas softly, "do you notice that all those thousands of apes gathered here in the arena apparently are paying no attention to us?"

"Yes, I noticed," replied the earthman. "They are all looking into the sky toward the city."

"Look," whispered Dejah Thoris. "It's the same thing on which the ape rode when he captured me in the Helium Forest after shooting our thoat!"

There appeared in the sky, coming from the direction of the city, a great, lone bird upon whose back rode a single man.

The earthman's keen eyes squinted for an instant. "The bird is a malagor. Pew Mogel is riding it."

The bird and its rider circled directly overhead.

"Open the east gate," Pew Mogel commanded, his voice ringing out through a loudspeaker somewhere in the arena.

The gates were thrown open and there began pouring out into the arena wave after wave of malagors exactly like the bird Pew Mogel rode.

As the malagors came out, column after column of apes were waiting at the entrance to vault onto the birds' backs.

As each bird was mounted, it rose into the air by telepathic command to join a constantly growing formation circling high overhead.

The mounting of the birds must have taken nearly two hours, so great were the numbers of Pew Mogel's apes and birds. Carter noticed that upon each ape's back was strapped a rifle and each bird carried a varying assortment of military equipment, including ammunition supplies, small cannon and a sub-machine gun was carried by each flight platoon.

At last all was ready and Pew Mogel descended down over the cages of his three captives.

"You see now Pew Mogel's mighty army," he cried, "with which he will conquer Helium and then all Barsoom." The man seemed very confident, for his crooked, misshapen body sat very straight upon his feathered mount.

"Before you are chewed to bits by the reptiles in the water below you," he said "you will have a few moments to consider the fate that awaits Helium within the next forty-eight hours. I should have preferred to conquer peacefully but you interfered. For that, you die, slowly and horribly."

Pew Mogel turned to the only ape that was left in the arena, the keeper of the key to the cages.

"Open the flood-gate!" was his single command before he rose up to lead his troops off toward the north.

Accompanying the weird, flying army in a sling carried by a hundred malagors rode Joog, the synthetic giant. A hollow, mirthless laugh pealed like thunder from the giant's throat as he was born away into the sky.

Chapter Eight: The Reptile Pit

As the last bird in Pew Mogel's fantastic army flapped out of sight behind the rim of the crater, John Carter turned to Tars Tarkas in the cage hanging beside him. He spoke softly so that Dejah Thoris would not hear.

"Those creatures will make Helium a formidable enemy," he said. "Kantos Kan's splendid airfleet and infantry will be hard pressed against those thousands of apes equipped with human brains and modern armament, mounted upon fast birds of prey!"

"Kantos Kan and his airfleet are not even in Helium to protect the city," announced Tars Tarkas grimly. "I heard Pew Mogel bragging that he had sent Kantos Kan a false message, supposedly from you, urging that all Helium's fleet, as well as all the ships of the searching party, be dispatched to your aid in the Great Toonolian Marshes."

"The Toonolian Marshes!" Carter gasped, "They're a thousand miles from Helium in the other direction."

A little scream from Dejah Thoris brought the men's attention to their own, immediate fate.

The ape beside the pit had pulled back a tall, metal lever.

There was a gurgle of bubbles as air blasted up from the water in the pit below the three captives and the water at the same time commenced to rise slowly.

The guard now unfastened the rope on each cage and lowered them so that the cage tops were a little below the surface of the ground inside the pit. Then he refastened the ropes and stood for some time on the brink looking down on the helpless captives.

"The water rises slowly," he sneered thickly, "and so I shall have time now for a little sleep."

It was uncanny to hear words issuing from the mouth of the beast. They were barely articulate, for although the human brain in the ape's skull directed the words, the muscles of the larynx in the creature's throat were normally unequipped for the specialized task of human speech.

The guard lay down on the brink and stretched his massive, squat body.

"Your death cries will awaken me," he mumbled pleasantly, "when the water begins to envelop your feet and the reptiles start clawing at you through the bars of your cages." Whereupon, the ape rolled over and began snoring.

It was then that the three captives saw the slanting, evil eyes, the rows of flashing teeth, in a dozen hideous, reptilian faces staring greedily up at them from the rising waters below.

"Quite ingenious," remarked Tars Tarkas, his stoic face giving no more evidence of fear than did that of the earthman. "When the water partly submerges us, the reptiles will reach in with their claws and begin tearing us to pieces--if there is any life left in us, the rising water will drown it out when finally it submerges the tops of our cages."

"How horrible!" gasped Dejah Thoris.

John Carter's eyes were fastened on the brink of the pit. From his cage he could just see one of the guard's feet as the fellow lay asleep at the edge of the pit.

Cautioning the others to silence, Carter began swinging his body back and forth while he held fast to the bars of the cage. If he could just get it swinging.

The water had risen to about ten feet below their cages.

It seemed an eternity before he could get the heavy cage to even moving slightly. Nine feet to the water surface and those hideous, staring eyes and those gleaming teeth!

The cage was swinging now a little more, in rhythm to the earthman's constantly swaying body.

Eight feet, seven feet, six feet came the water. There were about ten reptiles in the water below the captives--ten pairs of narrow, evil eyes fixed steadily to their prey.

The cage was swinging faster.

Five feet, four feet, Tars Tarkas and Dejah Thoris could feel the hot breath of the reptiles!

Three feet, two feet! Only two more feet to go before the steadily swinging cage would cut into the water and slow down to a standstill.

But the iron prison, swinging pendulum-like, would reach the brink on its next swing so this time as the cage moved toward the brink on which lay the sleeping guard, John Carter knew he must act quickly.

As the bars of the cage smacked against the cement wall of the pit, John Carter's arms shot out with the quickness of a striking snake.

His fingers closed in a grip of steel about the ankle of the sleeping guard.

An ear-piercing shriek rang out across the arena, echoing dismally in the hollow crater, as the ape felt himself jerked suddenly from his slumbers.

Back swung the cage. Carter regrasped the shrieking ape with his other hand through the bars as they swung out over the water. The reptiles had to lower their heads as the cage moved over them so close had the water risen.

"Good work, John Carter," came Tars Tarkas's tense words as he reached out and grabbed hold of the ape with his four mighty hands. At the same time, Carter's cage splashed to a sudden stop. It had hit the water's surface.

"Hold him, Tars Tarkas. While I pull the key off the scoundrel's neck-- there, I've got it!"

The water was flowing over the bottom of the cages. One of the reptiles had reached a horny arm in Dejah Thoris's cage and was attempting to snag her body with its sharp, hooked claws.

Tars Tarkas flung the ape's body with all the force of his giant thews straight at the reptile beside the girl's cage.

"Quickly, John Carter," cried Dejah Thoris. "Save yourself while they are fighting over the ape's body."

"Yes," echoed Tars Tarkas, "unlock your cage and get out while there is still time."

A half-smile lifted the corner of Carter's mouth as he swung open his prison door and leaped to the top of Dejah Thoris's cage.

"I'd sooner stay and die with you both," the earthman said, "than desert you now."

Carter soon had the princess' prison door unlocked but as he reached down to lift the girl up, a reptile darted forward into the cage with the princess.

In a quick second, Carter was inside the girl's cage, already knee-deep in water and he had hurled himself onto the back of the reptile. A steely arm was clamped tightly around the creature's neck. The head was jerked back just in time for the heavy jaws snapped closed only an inch from the girl's body.

"Climb out, Dejah Thoris--to the top of the cage!" ordered Carter. When she had obeyed, Carter dragged the flopping, helpless reptile to the cage door, as other slimy monsters started in. Using its body as a shield before him, the earthman forced his way to the door.

In an instant he had released his hold and vaulted up on top of the cage with the girl.

A moment later he had unlocked Tars Tarkas's cage door. After the green man had swung up beside them without mishap, the three climbed the ropes to the scaffolding above and then lowered themselves down to the ground beside the pit.

"Thank Issus," breathed the girl as they sat down to regain their breaths. Her beautiful head was cushioned upon Carter's shoulder, and he stroked her lovely black hair reassuringly.

Presently the earthman rose to his feet. Tars Tarkas had motioned him across the arena.

"There are some malagors left inside here," Tars Tarkas called from the entrance to the cavern inside the crater from where had come Pew Mogel's mounts.

"Good!" exclaimed Carter. "There may be a chance yet to reach and help Helium."

A moment later they had caught two of the birds and had risen over the ancient city of Korvas.

They spotted their planes on the outskirts of the city where they had left them the night they were tricked into being captured by Pew Mogel.

But to their disappointment, the controls had been destroyed irreparably, so they were forced to continue their journey on the backs of the malagors.

However, the malagors proved speedy mounts. By noon the next day the trio had reached the City of Thark, inhabited by a hundred thousand green warriors over whom Tars Tarkas ruled.

Gathering the warriors together in the marketplace, Tars Tarkas and John Carter explained the peril that confronted Helium and asked for their support in marching to their allies' aid.

As one man, the mighty warriors shouted their approval. The next day dawned upon a long caravan of thoat-mounted soldiers streaming out from the city gates towardsHelium.

A messenger was sent on a malagor to the Toonolian Marshes in an attempt to locate Kantos Kan and urge him to return home with his fleet to aid in the defense of Helium.

Tars Tarkas had abandoned his malagor to this messenger, in favour of a thoat upon which he rode at the head of his warriors. Directly above him, mounted on the other malagor rode Dejah Thoris and John Carter.

Chapter Nine: Attack on Helium

John Carter and Dejah Thoris, mounted upon their malagor, were scouting far ahead of the main column of advancing warriors when they first came in sight of the besieged City of Helium.

It was bright moonlight. The princess voiced a little, disappointed cry when she looked out across the spacious valley towards Helium. Her grandfather's city was completely surrounded by the besieging troops of Pew Mogel.

"My poor city!" The girl was crying softly, for in the bright moonlight below could be easily discerned the terrific gap in the ramparts and the many crushed and shattered buildings of the beautiful metropolis.

John Carter telepathically commanded the malagor to land upon a high peak in the mountains overlooking the Valley of Helium.

"Listen," cautioned John Carter. Pew Mogel's light entrenched cannon and small arms were commencing to open fire again by moonlight. "They are getting ready for an air attack."

Suddenly, from behind the two foothills between the valley and the towering peaks, there rose the vast, flying army of Pew Mogel.

"They are closing in from all sides," Dejah Thoris cried.

The great winged creatures and their formidable ape riders were swooping down relentlessly upon the city. Only a few of Helium's airships rose to give battle.

"Kantos Kan must have taken nearly all Helium's fleet with him," the earthman remarked. "I am surprised Helium has withstood the attack as long as this."

"You should know my people by now, John Carter," replied the princess.

"The infantry and anti-aircraft fire entrenched in Helium are doing well," Carter replied. "See those birds plummet to the ground."

"They can't hold out much longer, though," the girl replied. "Those apes are dropping bombs squarely into the city, as they swoop over, wave after wave of them--oh, John Carter, what can we do?"

John Carter's old fighting smile, usually present at times of personal danger, had given way to a stern, grave expression.

He saw below him the oldest and most powerful city on Mars being conquered by Pew Mogel's forces. Armed with Helium's vast resources, the synthetic man would go forth and conquer all the civilized nations on Mars.

Fifty thousand years of Martian learning and culture wrecked by a power-mad maniac, himself the synthetic product of civilized man!

"Is there nothing we can do to stop him, John Carter?" came the girl's repeated question.

"Very little, I'm afraid, my princess," he replied sadly, "All we can do is station Tars Tarkas's green warriors at an advantageous point in preparation for the counterattack and trust to fate that our messenger reached Kantos Kan in time that he may return and aid us."

"Without supporting aircraft, our green warriors, heroic fighters that they are, can do little against Pew Mogel's superior numbers in the air."

When John Carter and Dejah Thoris returned to Tars Tarkas, they reported what they had seen.

The great Thark agreed that his warriors could avail but little in a direct attack against Pew Mogel's air force. It was decided that half their troops be concentrated at one point and at dawn attempt to rush into the city.

The remaining half of the warriors would scatter into the mountains in smaller groups and engage the enemy in guerilla warfare.

Thus they hoped to forestall the fate of Helium until Kantos Kan returned with his fleet of speedy air fighters.

"Helium's fleet of trim, metal fighting craft will furnish Pew Mogel's feathered-bird brigade a worthy enemy," remarked Tars Tarkas.

"Provided, of course," added John Carter, "Kantos Kan's fleet reaches Helium before Pew Mogel has entrenched himself in the City and returned his own anti-aircraft guns upon them."

All that night in the mountains, under cover of semi-darkness, John Carter and Tars Tarkas reorganized and restationed their troops. By dawn, all was ready.

John Carter and Tars Tarkas would lead the advance half of the Tharks in a wild rush toward the gates of Helium, the other half would remain behind, covering their comrades' assault with long-range rifles.

Much against the earthman's will, Dejah Thoris insisted she would ride into the City beside him upon their malagor.

It was just commencing to grow brighter.

"Prepare to charge," John Carter ordered. Tars Tarkas passed the word down and across by his orderly to his unit commanders.

"Prepare to charge! Prepare to charge!" echoed down and across the battalions of magnificent, four-armed green fighters astride their eight-legged, massive, restless thoats.

The minutes dragged by as the troop lines swung around. Steel swords were drawn from scabbards. Hammers, on short deadly ray-pistols, clicked back as they cocked over saddle pommels.

John Carter looked around at the girl sitting so straight and steady behind him.

"You are very brave, my princess," he said.

"It's easy to be brave," she replied, "when I'm so close to the greatest warrior on Mars."

"Charge!" came John Carter's terse, sudden order.

Down the mountain and across the plain toward Helium streaked the savage hoard of Tharks. Out ahead raced Tars Tarkas, his sword held high.

Far ahead and above, on speedy wings, streaked the malagor bearing John Carter and the Princess of Helium.

"John Carter, thank Issus!" Dejah Thoris cried in relief and pointed toward the far mountain skyline.

"The Helium fleet has returned," shouted John Carter. "Our messenger reached Kantos Kan in time!" Over the mountains, with flying banners streaming, sailed the mighty Helium fleet.

There was a moment's silence in the entrenched guns of the enemy. They had seen the charging Tharks and the Helium fleet simultaneously.

A great cry of triumph rose from the ranks of the charging warriors at the sight of the Helium fleet streaking to their aid.

"Listen," cried Dejah Thoris to Carter, "the bells of Helium are tolling our victory song!" then it seemed as though all of Pew Mogel's guns broke loose at once and from behind the protecting hills rose his flying legions of winged malagors. Upon their backs rode the white apes with men's brains.

Down upon the legions of Tharks came wave after wave of Pew Mogel's feathered squadrons. In true blitzkrieg fashion, the birds would swoop down just out of sword's reach over the green warriors. As each bird pulled out of its dive, the ape on its back would empty its death-dealing atomgun into the mass of warriors beneath.

The carnage was terrific. Only after Tars Tarkas and John Carter had led their warriors into the first lines of entrenched apes did the Tharks find an enemy with whom they could fight effectively.

Here, the four-armed green soldiers of Thark fought gloriously against the great white apes of Pew Mogel's ghastly legions.

But never for a second did the horrible death-dealing squadrons cease their attacks from above. Like angry hornets, the thousands dove, killed, climbed again, always killing.

John Carter masterfully controlled his frightened bird while he issued orders and directed attacks from his vantage point immediately above the center of battle.

Bravely, efficiently, the Princess of Helium protected her chieftain against countless side and rear attacks from the air. The barrel of her radium pistol was red-hot with constant firing and many were the charging birds and shrieking apes she sent catapulting into the melee below.

Suddenly a hoarse shout rose again from Pew Mogel's legions on ground and in the air.

"What is it, my chieftain?" cried the girl. "Why are the enemy shouting in triumph?"

John Carter looked toward the advancing ships now over the mountains only half a mile away, then his blood ran cold.

"The giant--Joog the giant!"

The creature had risen up from behind the shelter of a low hill, as the ships approached above him. The giant grasped a huge tree trunk in his mighty hand.

Even from where they were, John Carter could discern the head of a man sitting in an armor-enclosed, steel howdah strapped to the top of Joog's helmet.

From the giant's lips there suddenly issued a thunderous, shrieking roar that echoed in the mountains and across the plain.

Then he clambered swiftly to the top of a small hill. Before the astonished Heliumites could swerve their speeding craft, the giant struck out mightily with the great tree trunk.

The great, synthetic muscles of Pew Mogel's giant swung the huge weapon full into the advancing craft.

The vanguard of twenty ships, the pride of Helium's airfleet met the blow head-on--went smashing and shattering against the mountain-side, carrying their crews to swift, crushing death!

Chapter Ten: Two Thousand Parachutes

Kantos Kan's flagship narrowly escaped annihilation at the first blow of the giant. The creature's club only missed the leading ship by a few feet.

From their position on the malagor, John Carter and Dejah Thoris could see many of the airships turning back toward the mountains. Others, however, were not so fortunate.

Caught in the wild rush of air resulting from the giant's swinging club, the craft pitched and tossed crazily out of control. Again and again the huge tree trunk split through the air as the giant swung blow after blow at the helpless ships.

"Kantos Kan is re-forming his fleet," John Carter shouted above the roar of battle as the fighting on the ground was once more resumed with increased zeal.

"The ships are returning again," cried the princess, "toward that awful creature!"

"They are spreading out in the air," the earthman replied. "Kantos Kan is trying to surround the giant!"

"But why?"

"Look, they are giving him some of Pew Mogel's own medicine!"

Helium's vast fleet of airships was darting in from all sides. Others came zooming down from above. As they approached within range of their massive target, the gunners would pour out a veritable hail of bullets and rays into the giant's body.

Dejah Thoris sighed in relief. "He can't stand that much longer!" she said.

John Carter, however, shook his head sadly as the giant began to strike down the planes with renewed fury.

"I'm afraid it's useless. Not only those bullets but the ray-guns as well are having no effect upon the creature. His body has been imbued with a serum that Ras Thavas discovered. The stuff spreads throughout the tissue cells and makes them regrow immediately with unbelievable speed to replace all wounded or destroyed flesh."

"You mean," Dejah Thoris asked, horror-stricken, "the awful monster might never be destroyed?"

"It is probable that he will live and grow forever," replied the earthman, "unless something drastic is done to destroy him."

A sudden fire of determination flared in the earthman's steel grey eyes.

"There may be a way yet to stop him, my princess, and save our people-"

A weird, bold plan had formulated itself in John Carter's mind. He was accustomed to acting quickly on sudden impulse. Now he ordered his malagor down close over Tars Tarkas's head.

Although he knew the battle was hopeless, the green man was fighting furiously on his great thoat.

"Call your men back to the mountains," shouted Carter to his old friend. "Hide out there and reorganize--wait for my return!"

The next half hour found John Carter and the girl beside Kantos Kan's flagship. The great Helium fleet had once more retreated over the mountains to take stock of its losses and re-form for a new attack.

Every ship's captain must have known the futility of further battle against this indomitable element; yet they were all willing to fight to the last for their nation and for their princess, who had so recently been rescued.

After the earthman and the girl boarded the flagship, they freed the great malagor that had so faithfully served them. Kantos Kan joyously greeted the princess on bended knee and then welcomed his old friend.

"To know you two are safe again is a pleasure that even outweighs the great sadness of seeing our City of Helium fall into the enemy's hands," stated Kantos Kan sincerely.

"We have not lost yet, Kantos Kan," said the earthman. "I have a plan that might save us--I'll need ten of your largest planes manned by only a minimum crew."

"I'll wire orders for them to break formation and assemble beside the flagship immediately," replied Kantos Kan, turning to an orderly.

"Just a minute," added Carter. "I'll want each plane equipped with two hundred parachutes."

"Two hundred parachutes?" echoed the orderly. "Yes, sir!" Almost immediately there were ten large aircraft, empty troop ships, drifting in single file formation beside Kantos Kan's flagship. Each had a minimum crew of ten men and two hundred parachutes, two thousand parachutes in all! Just before he boarded the leading ship, John Carter spoke to Kantos Kan.

"Keep your fleet intact," he said, "until I return. Stay near Helium and protect the city as best you can. I'll be back by dawn."

"But that monster," groaned Kantos Kan. "Look at him. We must do something to save Helium."

The enormous creature, standing one hundred and thirty feet tall, dressed in his ill-fitting, baggy tunic, was tossing boulders and bombs into Helium, his every action dictated through short wave by Pew Mogel, who sat in the armored howdah atop the giant's head.

John Carter laid his hand on Kantos Kan's shoulder.

"Don't waste further ships and men uselessly in fighting the creature," he warned "and trust me, my friend. Do as I say--at least until dawn!"

John Carter took Dejah Thoris's hand in his and kissed it. "Goodbye, my chieftain," she whispered, tears filling her eyes.

"You'll be safer here with Kantos Kan, Dejah Thoris," spoke the earthman; and then, "Goodbye, my princess," he called and vaulted lightly over the craft's rail to the deck of the troop ship alongside. It pained him to leave Dejah Thoris; yet he knew she was in safe hands.

Ten minutes later, Dejah Thoris and Kantos Kan watched the ten speedy craft disappear into the distant haze.

When John Carter had gone, Kantos Kan unfurled Dejah Thoris's personal colors beside the nation's flag; so that all Helium would know that their princess had been found safe and the people be heartened by her close presence.

During his absence, Kantos Kan and Tars Tarkas followed the earthman's orders, refraining from throwing away their forces in hopeless battle. As a result, Pew Mogel's fighters had moved closer and closer to Helium; while Pew Mogel himself was even now preparing Joog to lead the final assault upon the fortressed city. Exactly twenty-four hours later, John Carter's ten ships returned.

As he approached Helium, the earthman took in the situation at a glance. He had feared that he would be too late, for his secret mission had occupied more precious time than he had anticipated.

But now he sighed with relief. There was still time to put into execution his bold plan, the plan upon which rested the fate of a nation.

Chapter Eleven: A Daring Plan

Fearing that Pew Mogel might somehow intercept any shortwave signal to Kantos Kan, John Carter sought out the flagship and hove to alongside it.

The troop ships that had accompanied him on his secret mission were strung out behind their leader.

Their captains awaited the next orders of this remarkable man from another world. In the last twenty-four hours they had seen John Carter accomplish a task that no Martian would have even dreamed of attempting.

The next four hours would determine the success or failure of a plan so fantastic that the earthman himself had half-smiled at its contemplation.

Even his old friend, Kantos Kan, shook his head sadly when John Carter explained his intentions a few minutes later in the cabin of the flagship.

"I'm afraid it's no use, John Carter," he said. "Even though your plan is most ingeniously conceived, it will avail naught against that horrible monstrosity.

"Helium is doomed, and although we shall all fight until the last to save her, it can do no good."

As he talked, Kantos Kan was looking down at Helium far below. Joog the giant could be seen on the plain hurling great boulders into the city.

Why Pew Mogel had not ordered the giant into the city itself by this time, Carter could not understand--unless it was because Pew Mogel actually enjoyed watching the destructive effect of the boulders as they crashed into the buildings of Helium.

Actually, Joog, however frightful in appearance, could best serve his master's purpose by biding his time, for he was doing more damage at present than he could possibly accomplish within the city itself.

But it was only a matter of time before Pew Mogel would order a general attack upon the city.

Then his entrenched forces would dash in, scaling the walls and crashing the gates. Overhead would swoop the supporting apes on their speedy mounts, bringing death and destruction from the air.

And finally Joog would come, adding the final coup to Pew Mogel's victory.

The horrible carnage that would then fall upon his people made Kantos Kan shudder.

"There is no time to lose, Kantos Kan," spoke the earthman. "I must have your assurance that you will see that my orders are followed to the letter."

Kantos Kan looked at the earthman for some time before he spoke.

"You have my word, John Carter," he said, "even though I know it will mean your death, for no man, not even you, can accomplish what you plan to do!"

"Good!" cried the earthman. "I shall leave immediately; and when you see the giant raise and lower his arm three times, that will be your signal to carry out my orders!"

Just before he left the flagship, John Carter knocked at Dejah Thoris's cabin door.

"Come," he heard her reply from within. As he threw open the door, he saw Dejah Thoris seated at a table. She had just flicked off the visiscreen upon which she had caught the vision of Kantos Kan. The girl rose, tears filling her eyes.

"Do not leave again, John Carter," she pleaded. "Kantos Kan has just told me of your rash plan--it cannot possibly succeed, and you will only be sacrificing yourself uselessly. Stay with me, my chieftain, and we shall die together!" John Carter strode across the room and took his princess in his arms--perhaps for the last time. She pillowed her head on his broad chest and cried softly. He held her close for a brief moment before he spoke.

"Upon Mars," he said, "I have found a free and kindly people whose civilization I have learned to cherish. Their princess is the woman I love.

"She and her people to whom she belongs are in grave danger. While there is even a slight chance for me to save you and Helium from the terrible catastrophe that threatens all Mars, I must act."

Dejah Thoris straightened a little at his words and smiled bravely as she looked up at him.

"I'm sorry, my chieftain," she whispered. "For a minute, my love for you made me forget that I belong also to my people. If there is any chance of saving them, I would be horribly selfish to detain you; so go now and remember, if you die the heart of Dejah Thoris dies with you!"

A moment later John Carter was seated behind the controls of the fastest, one-man airship in the entire Helium Navy.

He waved farewell to the two forlorn figures who stood at the rail of the flagship.

Then he opened wide the throttle of the quiet radium engine. He could feel the little craft shudder for an instant as it gained speed. The earthman pointed its nose upward and rose far above the battleground.

Then he nosed over and dove down. The wind whistled shrilly off the craft's trim lines as its increased momentum sped it, comet-like, downward--straight toward the giant!

Chapter Twelve: The Fate of a Nation

Neither Pew Mogel nor the giant Joog had yet seen the lone craft diving toward them from overhead. Pew Mogel, seated inside the armored howdah that was attached to Joog's enormous helmet, was issuing attack orders to his troops by shortwave.

A strip of glass, about three feet wide, completely encircled the howdah, enabling Pew Mogel to obtain complete, unrestricted vision of his fighting forces below.

Perhaps if Pew Mogel had looked up through the circular glass skylight in the dome of his steel shelter, he would have seen the earthman's speedy little craft streaking down on him from above.

John Carter was banking his life, that of the woman he loved and the survival of Helium upon the hope that Pew Mogel would not look up.

John Carter was driving his little craft with bullet speed--straight toward that circular opening on top of Pew Mogel's sanctuary.

Joog was standing still now, shoulders hunched forward. Pew Mogel had ordered him to be quiet while he completed his last-minute command to his troops.

The giant was on the plain between the mountains and the city. Not until he was five hundred feet above the little round window did Carter pull back on the throttle.

He had gained his great height to avoid discovery by Pew Mogel. His speed was for the same purpose.

Now, if he were to come out alive himself, he must slow down his hurtling craft. That impact must occur at exactly the right speed.

If he made the crash too fast, he might succeed only in killing himself, with no assurance that Pew Mogel had died with him.

On the other hand, if the speed of his ship were too slow it would never crash through the tough glass that covered the opening. In that case, his crippled plane would bounce harmlessly off the howdah and carry Carter to his death on the battlefield below.

One hundred feet over the window!

He shut off the motor, a quick glance at the speedometer--too fast for the impact!

His hands flew over the instrument panel. He jerked back on three levers. Three little parachutes whipped out behind the craft. There was a tug on the plane as its speed slowed down.

Then the ship's nose crashed against the little window! There was a crunch of steel, a splinter of wood, as the ship's nose collapsed; then a clatter of glass that ended in a dull, trembling thud as the craft bore through the window and lodged part way in the floor of Pew Mogel's compartment.

The tail of the craft was protruding out of the top of the howdah, but the craft's door was inside the compartment.

John Carter sprang from his ship, his blade gleaming in his hand.

Pew Mogel was still spinning around crazily in his revolving chair from the tremendous impact. His earphones and attached microphone, with which he had directed Joog's actions as well as his troop formations, had been knocked off his head and lay on the floor at his feet.

When his foolish spin finally stopped, Pew Mogel remained seated. He stared incredulously at the earthman.

His small, lidless eyes bulged. He opened his crooked mouth several times to speak. Now his twisted fingers worked spasmodically.

"Draw your sword, Pew Mogel!" spoke the earthman so low that Pew Mogel could hardly hear the words. The synthetic man made no move to obey.

"You're dead!" he finally croaked. It was like the man was trying to convince himself that what he saw confronting him with naked sword was only an ill-begotten hallucination. So hard, in fact, did Pew Mogel continue to stare that his left eye behaved as Carter had seen it do once before in Korvas when the creature was excited.

It popped out of its socket and hung down on his cheek. "Quickly, Pew Mogel, draw your weapon--I have no time to waste!"

Carter could feel the giant below him growing restless, shifting uneasily on his enormous feet. Apparently he did not yet suspect the change of masters in the howdah strapped to his helmet; yet he had jumped perceptibly when Carter's craft had torn into his master's sanctuary.

Carter reached down and picked up the microphone on the floor.

"Raise your arm," he shouted into the mouthpiece.

There was a pause; then the giant raised the right arm high over his head.

"Lower arm," Carter commanded again. The giant obeyed. Twice more, Carter gave the same command and the giant obeyed each time. The earthman half smiled. He knew Kantos Kan had seen the signal and would follow the orders he had given him earlier.

Now Pew Mogel's hand suddenly shot down to his side. It started back up with a radium gun.

There was a blinding flash as he pulled the trigger; then the gun flew miraculously from his hand.

Carter had leaped to one side. His sword had crashed against the weapon knocking it from Pew Mogel's grasp. Now the man was forced to draw his sword.

There, on top of the giant's head, fighting furiously with a synthetic man of Mars, John Carter found himself in one of the weirdest predicaments of his adventurous life.

Pew Mogel was no mean swordsman. In fact, so furious was his first attack that he had the earthman backing around the room hard-pressed to parry the swift torrent of blows that were aimed indiscriminately at every inch of his body from head to toe.

It was a ghastly sensation, fighting with a man whose eye hung down the side of his face. Pew Mogel had forgotten that it had popped out. The synthetic man could see equally well with either eye.

Now Pew Mogel had worked the earthman over to the window. Just for an instant he glanced out. An exclamation of surprise escaped his lips.

Chapter Thirteen: Panic

John Carter's eyes followed those of Pew Mogel. What he saw made him smile, renewed hope surging over him.

"Look, Pew Mogel," he cried. "Your flying army is disbanding!"

The thousands of malagors that had littered the sky with their hairy riders were croaking hoarsely as they scattered in all directions. The apes astride their backs were unable to control their wild fright. The birds were pitching off their riders in wholesale lots, as their great wings flapped furiously to escape that which had suddenly appeared in the sky among them.

The cause of their wild flight was immediately apparent. The air was filled with parachutes, and dangling from each falling parachute was a three-legged Martian rat-every Martian bird's hereditary foe!

In the quick glance that he took, Carter could see the creatures tumbling out of the troop ship into which he had loaded them during his absence of the last twenty-four hours.

His orders were being followed implicitly.

The rats would soon be landing among Pew Mogel's entrenched troops.

Now, however, John Carter's attention returned to his own immediate peril.

Pew Mogel swung viciously at the earthman. The blade nicked his shoulder, the blood flowed down his bronzed arm.

Carter stole another glance down. Those rats would need support when they landed in the trenches.

Good! Tars Tarkas's green warriors were again racing out of the hills, unhindered now by scathing fire from an enemy above.

True, the rats when they landed would attack anything in their path; but the green Tharks were mounted on fleet thoats, the apes had no mounts. No malagor would stay within sight of its most hated enemy.

Pew Mogel was backing up now once more near the window. Out of the corner of his eye, Carter caught sight of Kantos Kan's airfleet zooming down towards Pew Mogel's ape legions far below.

Pew Mogel suddenly reached down with his free hand.

His fingers clutched the microphone that Cater had dropped when Pew Mogel had first rushed at him.

Now the creature held it to his lips and before the earthman could prevent it he shouted into it.

"Joog!" He cried, "Kill! Kill! Kill!"

The next second, John Carter's blade has severed Pew Mogel's head from his shoulders.

The earthman dived for the microphone as it fell from the creature's hands; but he was met by Pew Mogel's headless body as it lunged blindly round the room still wielding its gleaming weapons.

Pew Mogel's head rolled about the floor, shrieking wildly as Joog charged forward to obey his master's last command to kill!

Joog's head jerked back and forth with each enormous stride. John Carter was hurled roughly about the narrow compartment with each step.

Pew Mogel's headless body floundered across the floor still striking out madly with the sword in it's hand.

"You can't kill me. You can't kill me," shrieked Pew Mogel's head, as it bounced about "I am Ras Thavas's synthetic man. I never die. I never die!"

The narrow entrance door to the howdah had flopped open as some flying object hit against its bolt.

Pew Mogel's body walked vacantly through the opening and went hurtling down to the ground far below.

Pew Mogel's head saw and shrieked in dismay; then Carter managed to grab it by the ear and hurl the head out after the body.

He could hear the thing shrieking all the way down; then its cries ceased suddenly.

Joog was now fighting furiously with the weapon he had just uprooted.

"I kill! I kill!" he bellowed as he smacked the huge club against the Helium planes as they drove down over the trenches.

Although the howdah was rocking violently, Carter clung to the window. He could see the rats landing now by the scores, hurling themselves viciously at the apes in the trenches.

And Tars Tarkas's green warriors were there now, also. They were fighting gloriously beside their great, four-armed leader.

But Joog's mighty club was mowing down a hundred fighters at a time as he swept it close above the ground. Joog had to be stopped somehow!

John Carter dove for the microphone that was sliding around the floor. He missed it, dove again. This time his fingers held it.

"Joog--stop! Stop!" Carter shouted into the microphone. Panting and growling, the great creature ceased his ruthless slaughter. He stood hunched over, the sullen, glaring hatred slowly dying away in his eyes, as the battle continued to rage at his feet.

The apes were now completely disbanded. They broke over the trenches and ran toward the mountains, pursued by the vicious, snarling rats and the green warriors of Tars Tarkas.

John Carter could see Kantos Kan's flagship hovering near Joog's head.

Fearing that Joog might aim an irritated blow at the craft with its precious cargo, the earthman signalled the ship to remain aloft.

Then his command once again rang into the microphone. "Joog, lie down.

Lie down!"

Like some tired beast of prey, Joog settled down on the ground amid the bodies of those he had killed.

John Carter leaped out of the howdah onto the ground. He still retained hold of the microphone that was tuned to the shortwave receiving set in Joog's ear.

"Joog!" shouted Carter again. "Go to Korvas. Go to Korvas."

The monster glared at the earthman, not ten feet from his face, and snarled.

Chapter Fourteen: Adventure's End

Once again the earthman repeated his command to Joog the giant. Now the snarl faded from his lips and from the brute's chest came a sound not unlike a sigh as he rose to his feet once again.

Turning slowly, Joog ambled off across the plain toward Korvas.

It was not until ten minutes later after the Heliumite soldiers had stormed from their city and surrounded the earthman and their princess that John Carter, holding Dejah Thoris tightly in his arms, saw Joog's head disappear over the mountains in the distance.

"Why did you let him go, John Carter?" asked Tars Tarkas, as he wiped the blood from his blade on the hide of his sweating thoat.

"Yes, why," repeated Kantos Kan, "when you had him in your power?"

John Carter turned and surveyed the battlefield. "All the death and destruction that has been caused here today was due not to Joog but to Pew Mogel," replied John Carter.

"Joog is harmless, now that his evil master is dead. Why add his death to all those others, even if we could have killed him--which I doubt?"

Kantos Kan was watching the rats disappear into the far mountains in pursuit of the great, lumbering apes.

"Tell me, John Carter," finally he said, a queer expression on his face, "how did you manage to capture those vicious rats, load them into those troop ships and even strap parachutes on them?"

John Carter smiled. "It was really simple," he said. "I had noticed in Korvas, when I was a prisoner in their underground city, that there was only one means of entrance to the cavern in which the rats live--a single tunnel that continued back for some distance before it branched, although there were openings in the ceiling far above; but they were out of reach.

"I led my men down into that tunnel and we built a huge smoke fire with debris from the ground above. The natural draft carried the smoke into the cavern.

"The place became so filled with smoke that the rats passed out by the scores from lack of oxygen, for they couldn't get by the fire in the tunnel--their only means of escape. Later, we simply went in and dragged out as many as we needed to load into our troop ships."

"But the parachutes!" exclaimed Kantos Kan. "How did you manage to get those on their backs or keep them from tearing them off when the creatures finally became conscious?"

"They did not regain consciousness until the last minute," replied the earthman. "We kept the inside cabin of each troop ship filled with enough smoke to keep the rats unconscious all the way to Helium. We had plenty of time to attach the parachutes to their backs. The rats came to in midair after my men shoved them out of the ships."

John Carter nodded toward the disappearing creatures in the mountains. "They were very much alive and fighting mad when they hit the ground, as you saw," added the earthman. "They simply stepped out of their parachute harnesses when they landed, and leaped for anyone in sight.

"As for the malagors," he concluded, "they are birds--and birds on both Earth and Mars have no love for snakes or rats. I knew those malagors would prefer other surroundings when they saw and smelled their natural enemies in the air around them!"

Dejah Thoris looked up at her chieftain and smiled. "Was there ever such a man before?" she asked. "Could it be that all earthman are like you?"

That night all Helium celebrated its victory. The streets of the city surged with laughing people. The mighty, green warriors of Thark mingled--in common brotherhood with the fighting legions of Helium.

In the royal palace was staged a great feast in honor of John Carter's service to Helium.

Old Tardos Mors, the jeddak, was so choked with feeling at the miraculous delivery of his city from the hands of their enemy and the safe return of his granddaughter that he was unable to speak for some time when he arose at the dining table to offer the kingdom's thanks to the earthman.

But when he finally spoke, his words were couched with the simple dignity of a great ruler. The intense gratitude of these people deeply touched the earthman's heart.

Later that night, John Carter and Dejah Thoris stood alone on a balcony overlooking the royal gardens.

The moons of Mars circled majestically across the heavens, causing the shadows of the distant mountains to roll and tumble in an ever-changing fantasy over the plain and the forest.

Even the shadows of the two people on the royal balcony slowly merged into one.

Made in the USA
Middletown, DE
22 August 2018